What a **COLD** Needs

Barbara Bottner   Pictures by Chris Sheban

NEAL PORTER BOOKS
HOLIDAY HOUSE / NEW YORK

To Miranda and Brandon: the very sweetest snifflers —B.B.

Neal Porter Books

Text copyright © 2019 by Barbara Bottner

Illustrations copyright © 2019 by Chris Sheban

All Rights Reserved

Printed and Bound in July 2018 at Hong Kong Graphics Ltd., China.

The artwork was created using watercolor, colored pencil, and graphite.

Book design by Jennifer Browne

www.holidayhouse.com

First Edition

1 3 5 7 9 10 8 6 4 2

Library of Congress Cataloging-in-Publication Data

Names: Bottner, Barbara, author. | Sheban, Chris, illustrator.

Title: What a cold needs / Barbara Bottner ; pictures by Chris Sheban.

Description: First edition. | New York : Holiday House, [2019] | "Neal Porter

Books." | Audience: Ages 4-8. | Audience: K to grade 3.

Identifiers: LCCN 2018009008 | ISBN 9780823441723 (hardcover)

Subjects: LCSH: Cold (Disease)—Juvenile literature.

Classification: LCC RF361 .B68 2019 | DDC 616.2/05—dc23 LC record available at https://lccn.loc.gov/2018009008

A cold needs . . .

a comfy bed near a window.
It likes to listen to the chirping of the birds

and the tinkling of raindrops,
with a clear view of the sweet blue sky.

A cold needs warm socks,

Mom's soft hands,
Grandma's famous chicken soup,

a kiss from Grandpa's
gentle lips,

and plenty of Dad's
goofy jokes.

A cold likes velvety tissues to sneeze into,

and sometimes a little medicine helps.

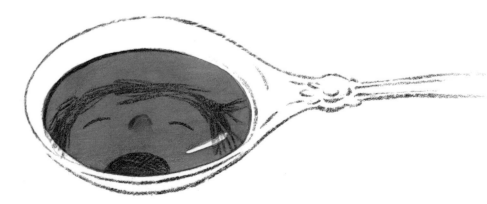

It likes music and a long,
deep afternoon nap.

A cold needs someone to say,
"Poor you."
And someone else who says,
"You'll feel better soon."

A cold needs to know that even
pesky sisters and brothers ask,
"How's she doing today?"

A cold needs a good book
with pictures of faraway places,

or a quiet game, a puzzle,
a little television,

and, if you're lucky,
Grandpa strumming
his guitar.

Sometimes a cold needs to be left alone.

A cold needs love,

and a little time,

until, finally, it says goodbye.

Then, once it's gone,
you get to run around
and cause just a little trouble and
do everything you love to do again,

and smile
that silly smile that
everyone's been waiting
to see.

A cold needs . . .

what a cold needs.